デイヴィッド・クリーガー詩集

神の涙

——広島・長崎原爆
国境を越えて

増補版

水崎野里子訳

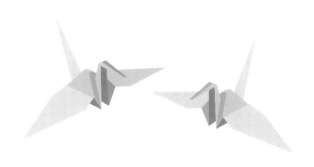

コールサック社

詩集 神の涙 —— 広島・長崎原爆 国境を越えて 増補版

デイヴィッド・クリーガー

水崎野里子訳

コールサック社
東京

著者略歴　デイヴィッド・クリーガー（David Krieger）

核時代平和財団の創立者、一九八二年から会長。アメリカ、ヨーロッパ、アジアで平和、安全保障、国際法、核兵器撤廃、地球温暖化の環境問題等について発言を続けている。世界平和と核廃絶活動により受賞多数。

著作は人類に対する核兵器の危険を幅広い視点から訴える。最新の詩集に『原爆の影の中で』（二〇一八年／アマゾン）。他に『今日は戦争に好い日ではない』（二〇〇五年／カリフォルニア・サンタバーバラ、カプラ出版）。

世界未来会議委員、多数の核時代平和活動団体の顧問。ハワイ大学より政治学で博士号（Ph.D.）、サンタバーバラ法律カレッジで法学博士（J.D.）。「核兵器廃絶国際キャンペーン」（ICAN）を組織・関与する団体の一員・活動家として二〇一七年にノーベル平和賞を受賞した。

6

はじめに

　私が最初に広島と長崎を訪れたのは大学を卒業した後の一九六三年であった。そ
れぞれの都市は平和記念資料館を造っていて原子爆弾による人間の苦しみを蘇ら
せる遺品を所持していた。この資料館で見た恐ろしい印象によって私は目ざめ、深
くこころを動かされた。多くの場合、人間の苦しみの物語は原子爆弾の使用につい
てアメリカで既に知られている伝承からは除外される。その伝承ははるかに単純で
ある──「我々は爆弾を落とした。戦争に勝った」。それは悲しいことだが科学技
術の勝利の物語であり続けている。

　平和資料館への訪問は私の目を開かせ、核兵器を明確に異なった視点で、はるか

7

に深い展望で眺める機縁となった。それは原爆の上にいた者たちと下にいた者たちの間に存在する巨大な差異への俯瞰を与えてくれた。この差異は、互いに並行する二つの宇宙とでも言えるほどの非常に大きな亀裂を形成し続けている。

原爆の上方の者たち、すなわち勝利者は彼らの武器の科学技術上の達成を祝った。彼らは次いで相互確証破壊に基づく核兵器競争に邁進するに至った。原爆の下方にいた者たちすなわち被害者は地獄の様相を目撃した。——爆風、焰、そして放射線——それらは爆弾の爆発の瞬時の化学反応によって造り出された。彼らは二つの原爆が死と破壊の結果をもたらすのを知った。そして勝利者とはるかに異なった教訓を学んだ——「二度と許すな！　悪をもはや繰り返すまい！」。

原爆の上方にいた者たちの抱く人類の未来像と下方にいた者たちのそれとは、現

8

在では決定的な相克を生じさせるかもしれない。科学技術の勝利者の側には権力の傲慢さがある。それはたやすく生命だけではなく文明の未来をも危険に曝す。生存者である被爆者の側には悪を悪と呼ぶ道徳的な明晰さがある。

科学技術上の「優位」と道徳的な明晰さとの間のこの争闘を解決することは安易ではない。科学技術は現代社会の中では主動力であったし威光の輝きを纏ってきた。インドとパキスタンがそれぞれ核兵器の実験をした一九九八年に一般民衆が街頭で喜びの祝いをした光景を核保有国の一員となる威光意識の証拠として私は鮮やかに今だに記憶している。

地球惑星上の多くの人々は核兵器に戸惑い、危険に対峙しようとする試みにおいて無力感を感じている。多くはまた無知か無関心か、あるいは考えようともしない。

9

不幸なことに、このような志向は現実では核兵器の人類への脅威の存続あるいは加速への票をすら投じる結果となる。唯一、核兵器に反対し核廃絶への活動に活発に参与することのみにより、個人は自らの見地と行動を原爆の下方にいる者たちすなわち広島と長崎の生存者たちと手をつなぎ合うことが出来る。その生存者たちは核時代に最も適した大使である。

私は何度も広島と長崎に戻って来た。そして私は常に被爆者の不屈の精神に勇気づけられて来た。時の経過によって彼らは今高齢となり、人類と核兵器とは共存し得ないという被爆者たちの強力な警告を拡げるには我々の助力と支援を必要としている。核兵器か人類の未来か、どちらかを選択しなければならないと主張する彼らの信念に私は同意したい。その選択は困難であるはずがない。

私達人類は核兵器を製造しそれらを抑制しようと試みて来た。私達は一九四五年の八月六日と九日にそれぞれ広島と長崎に落とされた原爆投下以来、戦役ではそれらを使用してはいない。六十五年が経過した。私達は幸運にも再度の世界の原子破壊への怒りを発せずに済んでいる。私達はこの幸運を讃えるべきである。だが満足すべきではない。今なおその勇気を表明することが私達すべての責任としてある。誇りを持って未来の世代に受け渡し得る世界を創造するために私達は核兵器の撤廃と廃絶を必要としているのだというその常識を今後も表明し続けなければならない。

デイヴィッド・クリーガー

カリフォルニア州サンタバーバラにて

＊「相互確認破壊 (Mutually Assured Destruction)」＝核兵器を保有する陣営のどちらか一方が相手に対し戦略核兵器を使用した際に、もう一方の陣営がそれを確実に察知し、報復を行う事により、一方が核兵器を使えば最終的にお互いが必ず破滅する、という状態のことを指す。互いに核兵器の使用をためらわせることを意図している。

12

I

原子爆弾

科学者たち

原子爆弾を最初に開発した科学者たちは互いに競い合っていた。あるいは少なくとも彼らはそう考えていた。だが一九四五年五月、欧州での戦争は終結しヒットラーは死んだ。彼らはヒットラー爆弾から世界を救おうとしていた。

科学者たちは彼らの製造物が日本に使用されるとは考えてはいなかった。彼らのうち何人か、たとえばレオ・シラードは、下方の人々を巻き込まない示威表示以外に原爆を使用することには懸命に反対した。何人かは原爆使用を支持した。だが日本が当時降伏を試みていることは彼らには知らされてはいなかった。科学者たちは世界の人々がかつて知ることのなかった最大級の力

を持つ爆弾を造った。そしてそれが造られた時、ちっぽけな政治家たちが担当となり原爆を送り出した。物語の教訓は以下である。「注意せよ、誰のために爆弾が造られたかを」。

15

レオ・シラード[*1]

きれいに後ろに梳られた黒い髪と最上の意図を持った奇妙な小男。ある日、君はロンドンで信号の赤い光を眺めながら待つ間に突然原爆を連想した。その爆発を想像して恐れおののき、君は友人のアインシュタインのところへ行き、それはヒットラーとの対戦用の爆弾であるように警告した。君はアインシュタインにルーズベルトに手紙を書くように依頼した。アインシュタインは書いた。それは始まりだった。

君はハッチンズ[*2]の大学では漂白員として勤務していた。君は君たちの考えに

16

ピカピカの金属の生命を与えるように助力した。だが彼らが既にそれを落下させようとしていると知った時、君の良心は驚愕した。君はトルーマンに手紙を書いた。トルーマンは君をバーンズ[*3]のもとに送り、バーンズは君を叱った。君は帰りの列車がゴトゴトと走ってゆく間、震え続けた。悪魔の子供は永遠に君の手に負えなくなったのだと理解しながら。

*1　レオ・シラード＝ハンガリー生まれの米国の物理学者（一八九八―一九六四）。

*2　ハッチンズ＝ロバート・メイヤード・ハッチンズ（一八九九―一九七七）。米国の教育家。シカゴ大学学長・名誉学長（一九二九―一九五一）。

*3　バーンズ＝ジェイムズ・フランシス・バーンズ（一八七九―一九七二）。米国の政治家・法律家。国務長官（一九四五―一九四七）。

17

トリニティのあと

未明の空を赤く照らした
トリニティ実験[*1]のあと　その週日
その巨大な白い火の玉に
オッペンハイマー[*2]の表情は暗かった

やがて次に何が起こるかを知っていた
彼はロスアラモス[*3]を歩き回った　目的もなく
パイプで煙草を吹かしながら　虚ろな目で

繰り返し　彼は呟いた
「哀れなちっぽけな人々よ
哀れなちっぽけな人々よ」

＊1　トリニティ実験＝一九四五年七月十六日五時二十九分にニューメキシコ州のソコロ実験場で行われた人類最初の核実験。爆縮型プルトニウム原子爆弾の爆発実験で、同型の爆弾が長崎市にやがて投下された。

＊2　オッペンハイマー＝ジュリウス・ロバート・オッペンハイマー（一九〇四─一九六七）。米国の理論物理学者。原子核物理学。世界最初の原爆製造の指導者。ロスアラモス研究所の初代所長。

＊3　ロスアラモス＝第二次大戦中の一九四三年にマンハッタン計画の中で原子爆弾の開発を目的として創設された、米国の国立研究機関であるロスアラモス国立研究所の所在地。ニューメキシコ州。

19

ポール・ティベッツ[*1]

君は操縦士、青二才、歯車の歯、兵士、そして爆撃兵だった。テニアン島[*2]から広島へ君は君の飛行機で歴史に飛び込んだ。ほとんど誰もが聞いたことのある有名な飛行機、エノラ・ゲイ、その名は君が君の母親にちなんで付けた。エノラ・ゲイはあの日広島にあの爆弾を運んだ。

君は誓った、君は高貴な大義に奉仕するアメリカの兵士たちの生命を救うと。他の者たちも、たとえばかつて太平洋で戦った、今では逝去の私の義父もそ

う考えた。深夜君は計画を変えることは考えもせずに、罪の意識もなく、どういう結果となるかも考えなかった。兵士たちの挨拶に君は挨拶した。エノラ・ゲイ機を操縦しつつ君は決して振り向かなかった。

＊1　ポール・ティベッツ＝ポール・ワーフィールド・ティベッツ（一九一五ー二〇〇七）。米空軍准将。B29爆撃機、エノラ・ゲイでテニアン島から飛び立ち、広島の上空で原子爆弾投下。ちなみに一九四五年八月には、彼は三十歳であった。

＊2　テニアン島＝西太平洋、マリアナ諸島南部に位置する島。サイパン島と共に日米の激戦地（一九四四年）であった。

21

ヒロシマ　一九四五年八月六日

空は澄んでいた　暑さと
約束で　刺すような空気
男達と女達は仕事に出掛けた
子供達は母親に挨拶「行ってきます」
爆弾が地上に向かって漂流していた間
街の人々は小股で歩いていた

22

狭い道路を　優美な橋を横切った

忘却に至る途中の道のり

爆弾の影は滑り去った　時間から

逃げ去った　爆音と爆風から

街を停止させた残酷な熱から

八月の朝

晴れた夏の朝――
「ロボット爆弾」は
ほんの一点　空の中で

ヒロシマ

ナガサキ

爆弾は粉砕する
蒸し暑い夏の沈黙を——
石の聖者たちの首を斬る

ヒロシマの四季

夏
静かな朝
突然　太陽が爆発する

秋
人々はさまよう
灰の中を

冬
太陽は無い
寒さが貫く

春
草が帰り来る
スモモの花

山端庸介

爆弾が長崎に落ちた日　君はそこにいた
カメラを持って　罪の証拠を捉えた

パチリ。　瀕死の赤ん坊が母親の乳を吸っている
母親の目は生気を失い　遠くを見つめている

パチリ。　呆然として女の子がおにぎりを持っている
その子の目はうつろで　顔は一面傷だらけ

パチリ。幼い少年の炭化した　硬直した死体が　大の字に

放り置かれる　固く乾いた地面に　黒焦げとなって

一方の手が自分の胸を摑んでいる　もう一方は

奇妙に曲がる　停止した彼の顔の表情

＊一九一七―一九六六年。日本の写真家。長崎市への原爆投下直後の一九四五年八月十日に陸
軍省西部報道部の指令で市内へ入り、被害の状況を撮影した。一九五二年、アメリカにおいて、
原爆を特集した「ライフ」誌（九月二十九日号）に写真が掲載された。一九五五年にはニューヨー
ク近代美術館で開催の写真展で彼の著名な原爆写真「おにぎりを持つ少年」が展示された。

短い歴史授業・一九四五年

八月六日。
原子爆弾落下
非戦闘員の上に
広島で

八月八日。
同意した

戦争犯罪の裁判
ナチスへの

八月九日。
原子爆弾落下
非戦闘員の上に
長崎で

神は涙で答えた

航空機は広島の上空を飛び　爆弾を落とした

緊急避難警報が鳴り渡った後だった

原子爆弾は落下した　光の速度よりずっと遅く

爆弾の速度で落下した

地上からは　それは小さな銀色の斑点だった

銀色の航空機から分離した

四十三秒後　ゆっくりと落ちる爆弾は炸裂し

火の玉と化した　光の二乗の速度で

アインシュタインはそれをエネルギーと呼んだ　すべては照り輝いた

一瞬　人々は自分の骨まで見えたほど

操縦士は常に信じた　正しいことを成し遂げたと

大統領も信念を揺るがせなかった

大統領は神に爆弾を感謝した　他の人々も同じだった

神は涙で答えた　涙は落下して行った

爆弾のスピードより　はるかにゆっくりと

涙は　いまだ地上に届かない

アイゼンハワーの意見

「彼らをそんな恐ろしいもので
攻撃する必要はなかった」
　　──ドワイト・D・アイゼンハワー司令官[1]

私達は彼らをそれで攻撃した　まず
広島で　次いで長崎で──
よく言う　ワン・ツー・パンチ

二つの爆撃は実験だったのさ　本当には

その「恐ろしいもの」の結果を見るための

爆縮型プラトニウム爆弾の[3]

まず銃型ウラニウム爆弾の[2]　次は

二つとも大いに効果的だった

二つの都市を抹殺する芸術においてはね

必要なかった

*1　ドワイト・D・アイゼンハワー（一八九〇～一九六九）＝米国の軍人、政治家。一九四二年

以降ヨーロッパ派遣米軍司令官、連合軍最高司令官を歴任。一九四五年陸軍参謀総長。

＊2　一九五二年から一九六一年まで第三十四代米国大統領。

＊3　銃型＝ガンタイプ核兵器とも言う。銃弾を他者に向けて発射する銃撃法を使用、武器内で一個の核分裂性ウラニウムを他端の核分裂性ウラニウムに向けて発射、両者を結合させて臨界超過質量に集結する。「リトルボーイ」の型。
爆縮型＝核分裂性物質を燃料として使用して（ウラニウム性、プルトニウム性、あるいは混合）その質量を凝縮させ、臨界状態を生じさせる。「ファットマン」の型。

36

その爆弾

その爆弾、金属製の目から落ちる涙、それは単なる爆弾ではない。

それは正気の降伏であり、暗黒と鎮圧へのあこがれである。

Ⅱ

生存者たち

下方の人々

街の中心で
市民は焼かれていた
燃える赤い周辺を持つ
その風の中の灰となった
もはや記憶は失われ
雲と共に漂流する
記憶と化した

周辺地区では
市民はより長く生きた
その瞬間の記憶は保たれた
彼らの骨と心臓の中に
それらはもろく悲しみと化した

生存者たちの嘆きは
力を尽くして思い出させた　私達に
その風の中の新しい構成分子を
だが　彼らの声はかすかで
忙しい時間だった　地球の上は

ゆるして　かあさん

沢田昭二*のために

あの爆撃のあと　若い少年は
目覚めた　部屋の瓦礫の下で
いまだ動けずにいた　崩壊した家の中で
母親の叫び声が聞こえた
彼は懸命に母親を助けようとした
でも　力が足らなかった

燃えさかる火が　二人に近づいて来た

多くの人々は急いで過ぎ去った

恐れおののき　人々は立ち止まらなかった

少年を助けようとはしなかった

瓦礫の下から　彼は母の声を聞いた

声はかすかだったがしっかりしていた

「逃げなさい　生きていてちょうだい」

彼女は言った　「私にかまわずに」

43

「ゆるして下さい」少年は言った　お辞儀をしながら

「ゆるして下さい　かあさん」

少年は母親が望んだように行動した

それは遠い昔のこと　一九四五年

少年はとうに大人になった　良い男に

でも彼はいまだに逃げ続けている　あの焔から

＊一九三一年生まれ。素粒子の理論物理学者。十三歳の時に広島で被爆。二〇〇七年に原爆投下に伴う残留放射線による内部被曝に関する論文を発表。

44

工芸品と灰

その工芸品の中に
炭化した焦げた死体があった

焦げた死体のひとつに
娘は見とどけた
母親の金歯

少女が手を伸ばし　焼かれた

遺体に触れようとすると
母親は崩れて灰となった

灰は少女の掌からさらさらと落ち
地面へと流れて行った

風が灰を運び去った
戦乱の絶えない世界の
いたるところに

被爆者の深いお辞儀

松原美代子*に

彼女は深くお辞儀をした。海よりも深く。富士山の頂上から海の底に至るほど深いお辞儀を。あまりにも深いお辞儀。何度も何度も。風は激しく吹いた。

風は吹き、彼女の小声の謝罪と祈りを五大陸すべてに運んだ。だが風は大声で叫びすぎたので、彼女の謝罪と祈りがよく聞き取れなかった。風は海を狂わせた。海水は盛り上がり、荒々しい分子の踊りを踊った。海は五大陸に押し寄せた。人々は恐れおののいた。彼らは岸辺から叫びながら逃げた。白い海水と叫ぶ風を懼れた。暗い場所に身を寄せ合った。耳を澄ませて風の中の

言葉を聞いた。

と思った人々もいた。

ある場所では謝罪を聞いたと思った人々もいた。　他の場所では祈りを聞いた

彼女は深いお辞儀をした。　誰よりも深く。

＊一九三二―二〇一八年。広島市出身。被爆者の一人。国内と国外における反核運動に生涯携わった。みずからアメリカ・カナダをはじめとする世界各国を回り、被爆体験を証言し、反核を訴えた。のち、インターネット使用。

49

おばあちゃんの語り

おばあちゃんは見つめた
孫娘の目を　原爆が広島に落とされた
その日を思い出しながら

空は真っ青だったの　彼女は言った
そしてね　空が爆発したとき
爆風で私は身体ごと吹っ飛んじゃった

私のまわりは　叫び声ばかり

いまでも耳にこだましている

母親を探し求める子供達

ぶら下がるリボンのようだった

虚ろなまなざし　皮膚は剥がれ

歩いて過ぎて行った負傷した人々

広島は死の都市となった

私達はみんな生きる意志を失ってしまった

でもやがて　草は新しい芽を出した

新しい芽と一緒に　暗黒は溶け去り

希望の小さな緑の葉となった

51

原爆の人々

それは始まった恐怖から　飢餓からではない
欠けていたものは生じた結果への理解だった
いまだに空は青い純真さを保っていた
それはずいぶんと前のこと
強烈な光が皮膚を貫いて
骨が見えるようになるずっと以前

貯蔵庫はまだ穀物を貯蔵していた

ミサイルではなく

雪を頂いた山々は空を掃き超然と聳えていた

原爆は戦争を終わらせたかもしれない

だが　歴史が遠い星のように読まれさえすればのこと

もしも時間があわてて進路を変えさえしなかったら

もしも白旗が翻りさえしたら　奇妙な嵐の前に

もしも空が白く老いさえしていなかったら

もしも一人のアインシュタインがいなくて

もう一人のヴォネガットがいたら*

＊ヴォネガット＝カート・ヴォネガット、米国の小説家（SF小説）、エッセイスト、劇作家（一九二二─二〇〇七）。代表作に『猫のゆりかご』、『スローターハウス5』（一九六九）など。インディアナ州でドイツ系四世として生まれる。一九四四年、アメリカ合衆国一〇六歩兵師団の兵士として欧州戦線に配属された。バルジ（アルデンヌ、ベルギー）の戦いで捕虜となり、連れて行かれたドレスデンで連合国軍（英米の空襲部隊）によって行われたいわゆる「ドレスデン大空襲」（一九四五年二月十三日から十四日。ドレスデン市街の八十五パーセントが壊滅、市民を含む死傷者は十万人とも十五万人とも推定されている）を経験した。その経験は「スローターハウス5」で主題化された。　母は一九四四年に自殺。

54

アインシュタインの後悔

アインシュタインの後悔は
深く流れる　悲しみの池
それは彼の目

彼のこころは見た
彼だけに見えるものを
曲がる光

速度を弱める時間
夜に過ぎゆく列車と
エネルギー量との関係

眠り　睡眠
目覚めることは可能だ
だが　誰が目覚める?

彼は見た　型を
降る雪に星に
想像を絶した単純性

ヒットラーの影が

ヨーロッパに拡がったとき

彼は何をすべきだった？

それは彼の目

より深く流れる　悲しみの池よりも

アインシュタインの後悔は　深い

犠牲者はどこへ行った？

犠牲者はどこへ行った？　まず最初に大気の中へ、次いで水の中へ、草木の中へ、最後にはわれわれの食べ物の中に行ったのだ。私は広島と長崎で焼かれた犠牲者について語っている。彼らは爆心地の近隣にいて私達の新しいエネルギーの熱と焔の中に捕らえられた。私は焼かれて構成分子に、他の原子に似た原子に化して大気に解き放たれて漂い、意志を失ったまま降下した犠牲者について語っている。

これは何を意味するのか？　私達は毎日の食事でその苦さを味わうことなく

60

私達の犠牲者を呼吸し、飲み、食べていることを意味する。そうとわからない方法でだがいやおうなく、私達が破壊した犠牲者と化す他に生きる術はないということを意味する。

広島の踊り

よろめくステップ
君は子供になった
少女に　母親に
未亡人に　葬儀の参列者に
君はつまずき転んだ
君は立ち上がり
翼を生やし飛び去った

私は君の踊りを見つめた

君の恐怖　怒り

君の若さと魔術

私は君が立ち上がるのを見た

灰の中から　飛んだ

鶴の翼で

そして大地に漂い降りた

63

死と化す

「いまや私は死、世界の破壊者となった」

——バガバッド・ギーター[*1]

オッペンハイマーが「今や私は死と化した」と考えた時、彼は「今や私達は死と化した」との意図であったのか？　オッペンハイマー[*2]が考えていたのは自分のことだったのか、私達すべてについてだったのか？

一九四五年のあの八月、トルーマンと彼の部下の兵士たちは二つの世界を破

64

壊した。彼らは理解しようとはしなかった、彼らが破壊した世界の中には自分たちの世界も含まれていたのだと。

アラモゴード*3から広島へはちょうど三週間かかった。八月六日にオッペンハイマーは再び死と化した。グローヴズ*4もスティムソンもバーンズ*5も同じだった。トルーマンも。あの日の広島での十万の人々も。アメリカも同じだった。

「これは歴史上最も偉大な事である」とトルーマンは言った。彼はあの日、自分が死と化したとは考えなかった。私達アメリカ人は勝つ方法を知っていた。トルーマンは勝利者であり世界の破壊者であった。三日後、トルーマンと兵士たちは再び長崎でそれを繰り返した。

65

その後少し経てオッペンハイマーはトルーマンを訪問した。「私の手は血で染まった」とオッペンハイマーは言った。トルーマンはその言葉が好きではなかった。

血？　なんの血？　オッペンハイマーが去ったとき、トルーマンは言った。「ここに彼を二度と入れてはならん」。

*1　バカバッド・ギーター＝ヒンドゥー教。インドの二大叙事詩のひとつ、マハーバーラタの一部。バラモン的な要素と他の要素を統合する宗教哲学詩。

*2　19ページ*2参照。

*3　アラモゴード＝米国ニューメキシコ州南部の都市。一九四五年七月に世界初の原爆実験が市の北西八十キロメートルの砂漠で行われた。

*4　グローヴズ＝レスリー・リチャード・グローヴズ（一八九六－一九七〇）。米国の将軍。

66

＊5　スティムソン＝ヘンリー・ルイス・スティムソン（一八六七－一九五〇）。米国の政治家。
国務長官（一九二九－三三）、陸軍長官（一九一一－一三、四〇－四五）。

第二次世界大戦中のマンハッタン計画の責任者。

被爆者は偶然の出来事ではない

あらゆる被爆者には
操縦士がいる

あらゆる被爆者には
計画者がいる

あらゆる被爆者には
爆撃手がいる

あらゆる被爆者には
爆弾設計者がいる

あらゆる被爆者には
ミサイル製造者がいる

あらゆる被爆者には
照準手がいる

あらゆる被爆者には
指揮官がいる

あらゆる被爆者には
ボタンを押す者がいる

あらゆる被爆者に
多くの者が貢献すべきだ

あらゆる被爆者に
多くの者が従うべきだ

あらゆる被爆者に
多くの者は口をつぐむべきだ

Ⅲ

思い出

広島平和記念資料館にて

一九四五年八月の広島市街の縮小模型は原爆が島病院の六〇〇メートル上空で爆発したことを示している。標的とした相生橋から三〇〇メートル南東の地点であった。その射程には本川小学校と伝福寺、妙法寺、常圓寺、誓願寺など五つの仏教寺があった。資料館の中を歩いて行くと、青い制服を着た日本の生徒たちがおしゃべりをしていた。一人の若い少年が同級生に言った。

「みんなずっと昔の出来事だったんだ」。

広島に落下されたその爆弾をどう呼ぼうか？

それを呼ぼうか
白い閃光の作成器具　あるいは
キノコ雲の作成用具？

それを呼ぼうか
戦争爆弾の終結用具　あるいは
人間兵器の火葬道具？

それを呼ぼうか

秘密勝利武器　あるいは

暗影露呈爆弾？

それを呼ぼうか

孤児作成爆弾？

若い兵士救済武器　あるいは

それを呼ぼうか　世界の

終わりの始まり　あるいは

始まりの終わり？

禎子と尺八 *

私達が広島を思い出すのは過去のためではなく未来のためである。私達が広島を思い出すのは広島の過去が私達の未来になってはならないからである。

広島を思い出したいと思うなら尺八という竹笛の簡素な音を聴くがいい。尺八はあの日の荒廃、破壊、街を覆った空虚を呼び戻す。尺八は涙をそそる。

涙は人間性を形作っている属性である。その人間性はあの爆弾で引き裂かれてしまった。

核兵器は武器などではない。人間の精神内破の象徴である。人間の尊厳の空

気を燃やし尽くす焔である。科学が悪と愛の欠如と手を握る十字路である。

それは戦争抑止という二枚舌の嘘に包まれた学問上の確信の勝利でしかない。

それはアインシュタインの後悔であった。それは他もろもろのものである。

だがもはや武器の次元ではない。もはや単なる戦争の道具ではなく、大量虐殺と生物全滅の道具である。

広島と禎子の物語を語り直し耳を傾けようと集まる人々はひとつの共同体である。人類の未来に参与した共同体である。私達は互いに互いを知らないかもしれない。だが私達は共同体である。広島を希望へと導くため、今日の祝典を祝うために世界中から集まった、より大きな共同体の一部である。

もし私達が継続すれば千羽鶴の禎子は新たな世代によって記憶され続けるで

あろう。彼女は人々の記憶の中にとどまり続けるであろう。その爆弾を製造し使用した人々の名と魂が尺八の心に染み入る音の中へと消え去った後も、長く。

＊禎子＝佐々木禎子（一九四三─一九五五）。広島平和記念公園内にある「原爆の子の像」のモデル。彼女は一九五五年十一月八日に原爆症で亡くなった。新聞で彼女の死を知った一青年によって原爆で死んだ子の像を建立しようと募金活動が始まり、一九五八年五月五日に建立。像は少女が折り鶴を天に掲げる形。像の周囲は千羽鶴で囲まれている。彼女は広島に原爆が投下された時二歳で爆心地から一・七キロメートルの自宅で黒い雨により被爆した。その後彼女は元気に成長したが、一九五四年末ごろ発病、白血病と診断され入院、一年後に死亡。入院中、彼女は折り紙や薬の包み紙などで折り鶴を折った。生前に彼女が折った鶴は一千三百羽とも一千五百羽とも言われる。

夢の庭

私が行く時、悲しい街よ、君も私と共に行く。

君はパリやローマのように俗っぽくはない。

私もそうだ。

君は頂上が雪で覆われた街ではなく

回りを静かな海で抱かれた街でもない。

そのような街はひとのこころを変えはしない。

君はニューヨークやデリーやリオとも違っている

ごったがえす人混みと都会の喧噪はない。

80

騒音と光とあわただしさは
君にはあまりにもはかない存在。

君の遺産は名誉あるものだ。それは
貴重で重要だ。悲劇のあと
君は君の大地を爪で耕し続け
やがて草木がゆっくりと戻って来た。
君は死から立ち戻った勇気を持った街。
君の市民は深くお辞儀をしそして微笑む
だが悲しい微笑みだ。

広島よ　悲しい街　私は君に贈る

81

私の孤独の強烈さを。

私は君に贈る　私の心の太鼓の連打を。

私は君を運ぶ　希望を持って

いつの日か君の精神からよりよい世界が花咲くであろう。

私は君に贈る　塩辛い私の涙を

君の悲嘆と未来とに混ぜ合わせてくれたまえ。

広島、君は夢の庭だ

私は庭師だ

君に負けない夢の庭師だ。

空に響け

「今日長崎の鐘よ空にこだませよ……」
——故長崎市長　伊藤一長

長崎の空はつらく、青く、不屈で未来の約束を抱いている。街は私達をやさしく迎えるがかつては原爆の標的となった。雲が開いて隙間を作り破壊の惨劇が起こった。でも誰もが予期しないうちに花々が戻って来た。記憶は痛々しく時には耐えられない。謝罪の言葉はやっては来なかった。生存者たちは老いて力を失った。世代は遷る。海上の空は悲しみに満ちている。長崎の鐘

よ響き渡れ、平和のために。空にこだませよ。

長崎の鐘

長崎の鐘*は
苦しんだ者のために鳴る
そしていまだ苦しむ者のために

鐘の音は引きつける　老いた女を
愛に輝く目をした
若い二人を

誘う　幼い子供達を

懸命に歩いて行く

爆心地へ向かって

長崎の鐘の音は

流れゆく　河のように

鳴れ　私達すべてのために　鳴れ

降りしきる落ち葉のように

＊長崎の鐘＝長崎平和公園内に昭和五十二年七月二十日に遺族や被爆者たち有志の呼びかけにより建立された。碑文には「長崎の鐘よ鳴れ」で始まる詩が刻まれている。また浦上天主堂のかつての「アンジェラスの鐘」として知られた大小二個の鐘は、大きい鐘は爆撃によって塔から転がり出たが破壊を免れた。小さい方の鐘はほぼ二つに割れた。割れた鐘はそのままの形で現在、浦上天主堂内に展示されている。永井隆博士により「アンジェラスの鐘」は「長崎の鐘」と命名された。

87

爆心地の早朝　長崎・二〇〇二年十一月十八日

十一月の朝の空気は冷たい
オレンジ色と黄色の葉が転がり落ちる
きれいに積まれた赤煉瓦の上を
どんよりと曇った朝　静かで寒い
落ち葉を掃き集め　まとめる
近くの芝生では管理係の老人たちが
私は立つ　爆心地の前に

黒一色の碑
空に屹立する

その五百メートル上空で
爆弾は身震いした
そして目覚めの　遠い昔

石碑の下には花々
近くでは　色とりどりの折り紙の鶴が
垂れ下がる　何羽もしっかりと束ねられて

＊長崎平和公園内には赤煉瓦を積み重ねて建立されたかつての浦上天主堂遺産（一部を移築）、
原爆落下中心碑（碑の高さ約六・五メートル、黒い直立の塔。塔の前には同じ黒石で箱型の
奉安箱が置かれ、犠牲者の名を刻んである）がある。

その爆弾が私達の神と化したとき

その爆弾が私達の神と化した時
私達はそれをあまりにも愛しすぎた
唯一の神とまで崇拝した

私達は自分たちを偉大で
強力　世界の創造主と考えた

私達は無限を志向した

その爆弾に魂まで与えてしまった

私達は慰めを期待した

その滑らかな金属製の恩恵に

その爆弾が私達の神と化した時

私達は生きていた　絶えない戦争の中で

私達はそれを平和と呼んだ

身を伏せ覆え――一九五〇頃

子供達！
こうすれば君たちは核攻撃から
助かる　警鐘が聞こえたらすぐさま
机の下に隠れろ　顔が床に届くような
姿勢でひざまづけ　そして頭を両腕で
保護するんだ　押さえつけて
いるままで両目は固く閉じておけ
開けてはいけない　見上げても　私が

「警報解除」と言うまで。

こうすれば君たちは助かる

一時間に数マイルの

速度で飛んで来る

ガラスや物体の破片から

君たちの眼球を溶かす白い

閃光から　君たちの脳や器官を

掻き乱して爆発からも

こうすれば君たちは助かる

君たちの生命を奪い　縮ませ

炭化させ　焼却してしまう焔から。

こうすれば君たちは助かる

放射能から　それを浴びると歯茎の出血

脱毛　白血病の原因となる　そしてやがて

死んでしまう　長いこと痛みに耐えた

挙げ句の死か　より短い期間での痛ましい死かだ

私の指示をしっかりと聞いておけ

その通りやるんだ　初めての時には。

核兵器発射将校がどう行動すべきか

私は命じられた場合以外には核兵器を発射しません。

私は命じられた際には鍵を回します。たとえ何名死ぬことになろうとも。

私はミサイル格納庫に坐っています。自分のことなど考えません。

私は核兵器が無差別殺人を起こし、同じく無差別の物件破壊者であることには無関心です。

私は国際法の下での私の義務は無視します。ニュルンベルク原則[*]も含めて。

私は進んで（標的となる国の名を記入せよ）を全滅させることにより、良い（好きな名詞を記入せよ）であることを証明します。

＊ニュルンベルク原則＝国連の国際法委員会によって作成された戦争犯罪を明文化する原則である。第二次大戦後、一九四五年八月八日の連合軍協定に基づき設立された国際軍事裁判所が同年十一月二十日にドイツ側の戦争犯罪者処罰のために開廷したニュルンベルク裁判の基礎となる法体系である。「平和に対する罪」「戦時犯罪」「人道に反する罪」「共同謀議」が言及され、国際法違反として明文化されている。ニュルンベルクは、ドイツ、バイエルン州の北部の都市。

平行する二つの宇宙

「もし私が知っていさえしたら
時計屋になっていただろう」
——アルバート・アインシュタイン

平行する一方の宇宙の中で
アインシュタインは仕事台に坐り
時計を作っている

光はいまだ大量の死体で曲折する

だが　彼はそれについては何も知らない

ただ時計を作っている　ひたすら　正確に

Ⅳ

挑

戦

核兵器廃絶のための十の理由

無差別長距離殺人用機械であり、兵士と非戦闘員、老人と新生児、男性と女性、そして子供を区別出来ない。

都市や国々や文明の破壊の脅威である。聖なるものすべて、人間的なものすべて、存在するものすべてを破壊する。

人類の未来への脅威である。

核兵器の所持者は卑怯者であり、その使用においては人間らしさも名誉も有り得ない。

偽の神であり、核を「持つ」国と「持たざる」国とに分け、保証され得ない威光と特権を核保有国に寄与している。

科学と工業技術との誤使用であり、私達の自然の知識を破壊目的へと歪曲している。

国際法を無視している。国際法の代わりに粗野な権力への忠誠を誓っている。

私達の資源を人類全滅のための道具の開発に浪費している。

権力誇示だけに専心し、民主主義を腐食している。

私達の人間性を堕落させている。

最後の句読点？

科学者は述べる、宇宙は約百五十億年前に宇宙大爆発によって創造されたと。この巨大な時間の拡がりを表現するには、私達は一万五千頁の本を想像すればよい。それはとても大きく重い本で、普通の本の五十倍ほどの大きさとなろう。本の中での一頁にはそれぞれ宇宙の歴史の中での百万年が書かれていることになる。一頁ごとに一千語を費やせば、一語は一千年を表すことになる。

本の大部分は宇宙大爆発以後の宇宙の拡大について書かれることになろ

う。私達の太陽系は一万五百頁で初めて出現することになる。最初の原始的な生命の形が約四十億年前に地球上に出現するまでには更に五百頁必要であ
る。生命のゆっくりとした進化にはほとんど本の終わりまで頁を占めるだろ
う。一万四千九百九十七頁で初めて人間の形をした生物が地球上に出現する。
そして一万五千頁の終わりのたった十語で初めて人類の文明が出現する。

一九四五年に始まった核時代は最後の終止符、すなわち一万五千頁の最後
の頁の句読点で表すことになる。巻末の最後のこの小さな点は、今日私達が
どこにいるかを指し示すだろう。私達は百五十億年の歴史の継承者としてい
る。同時に私達自身と他の生命体の大部分を科学技術の達成によって破壊し
てしまう能力を持つ。その最後の頁がめくられ、私達が安全に未来へと移行
すること、それを確実に保証するのが私達の責任である。未来、すなわち人

107

類とすべての生命体が現在曝されている、核兵器の脅威から解放された未来である。

想像力と核兵器

アインシュタインは知識には限界があるけれども想像力には限界はないと信じました。

　想像してください。数億人の死者を伴う核戦争の悲惨な現実を。ヒロシマのグローバル化であります。破壊された都市は炎上し、黒い煤に遮断され、温かい太陽は届きません。暗黒が世界全体を覆いつくし、気温は新たな氷河期にまで低下し、作物は収穫出来ず、人々は飢餓に陥ります。

核兵器は危機一髪の発射危機の状態にあり、核抑止策は限りない効果があるという、常に揺れ続ける仮定によって正当化されてしまうこと、これは簡単に想像出来ます。

その意味では、我々の想像力は変革への強力な機動力となり得ます。

現代の世界では、核兵器と相変わらず続く核脅威に満ちており、私たちは危うい核戦争勃発の崖っぷちに立っております。この危機は核兵器廃絶処理開始作業の不足ゆえでもあります。さらに、私たちは非常に幸運にも核戦争勃発の境を越えることを避けて来ているということ、そして核蔵庫を近代化するために、盲目的に、違法なほどの金額を注ぎ続けているからです。一方では、それゆえに、世界の人口の大部分を占める人々の生活の基礎となる需

111

要を満たせずにいるのです。

このジレンマから脱出する唯一の道は、世界の指導者たちに正気に戻ってもらい、核兵器が再び使用されないために、核兵器の廃止を合意してもらうことです。ですが私たちが現在住んでいる世界の状況を見てみれば、これはそんなに簡単に想像できることではないわけです。

核廃絶の目的を現実化するには、どんな手段が必要なのでしょうか？

第一に、核兵器禁止の条約が必要でしょう。この種の条約は２０１７年に国際連合加盟の指導的な国々によって合意されました。核兵器禁止条約です。この条約は今、合意される途上にあり、五十ヶ国によって合意されれば批准

112

されることになります。ですが、不幸なことに、また予想されたように、九ヶ国の核兵器所有国はこの条約を支持してはおりません。多くは公然と本条約に敵対して来ました。

　第二には、粘り強い話し合いが、九カ国の核兵器保有国すべてを含める世界の国々によって、核兵器廃絶の開始のために必要だということです。核兵器拡散禁止条約は既に信頼の置ける話し合いの場を設けることを同盟国に義務づけております。特に、本条約は、早期に核兵器製造競争を終わらせ、核兵器撤廃を成就させるように話し合いの場を要求しております。でも核兵器拡散禁止条約が施行になった一九七〇年以降、核兵器保有国は核兵器拡散禁止条約明記の義務を果たしてはおりません。

第三には、話し合いの場は、世界的な完全な核兵器撤廃の結果を包括すべく拡大されるべきであります。それは核廃絶が因習的な武器所有競争と戦争へ導かれることを許さないためであります。再び申し上げますが、核兵器拡散禁止条約に明記の国々は、信頼を持って話し合いの場を設ける義務があります。ですが、この義務は今だかつて一度も具現されてはおりません。

もし私たちが想像力を駆使して核戦争の恐怖を予見すれば、このような悲劇が起こらないように必要な手段を講じることが出来るに違いありません。ですがその手段は既に前述の二つの条約によって提示されているのです。

一貫して欠けているものは、二つの条約を補填する政治的な意志です。政治的に強力な意志がなければ、われわれの想像力にもかかわらず、起こりう

114

る核戦争の大惨事の舞台から逃れられないでしょう。核戦争は悪意、狂気、誤算、間違い、あるいはコンピューター操作（ハッキング）によって起こり得ます。想像力は必要です。しかし政治的な意志を克服するには十分ではありません。二つの条約さえも、彼らが準備した約束を実行させる政治的な意志がない限りは十分ではありません。十分であるためには、想像力は政治的な意志の変革を望む行動に繋がらなければなりません。

時間は短いです。仕事は重大です。私たちが核戦争勃発の持続する危機から逃れられない限り、恐ろしい結末は予測可能です。

立ち上がりましょう。

大統領

彼は
最初の大統領ではない
嘘と　間違いだらけの　政治家
でも　全く　見事に　達人

図々しくも　自分中心
エゴに餌　ポケットに詰め込む
巨大な報酬

偏狭な人種に安全な世界を作り

偏見の　酒樽の

栓を　大きく開けた

貧しい者たちに

荒々しく　波を浴びせ　さらに

自由の淑女から名誉を剥がした

彼は叫ぶ　「偽のニュースだ」　そして

名声を勝ち得ようと　民衆の飼い葉桶に立つ

こんな大統領は　前代未聞だ

117

毎日　新たな失策

でも　なんとか　どうにか

持ちこたえて来た

すべての独裁者のように　彼はいつか

倒されるだろう　だが　その時　我々に

いまだ　国は　世界はあるのか？

V

地球破壊の脅威と核廃絶

講演録　核兵器による地球破壊の脅威と核廃絶

長崎に再びおりますことは非常な喜びです。皆様の美しい市に私達を温かくお迎えいただき感謝します。私はいつも長崎に原爆が落とされた偶然性にこころ打たれます。あの運命の日標的は別の都市、小倉でした。ですが雲で覆われていて小倉は爆撃を免れたのです。もしあの雲がなかったら長崎は原爆を免れたでしょう。もし長崎市上空の雲に切れ目がなかったら長崎は原爆を免れたでしょう。雲のようにありきたりのものが根本的に私達の人生を変え得るのです。ですがそれは世界平和を築こう、地球惑星から核兵器を廃絶しようとする私達の行動も同じです。

ここ数年間私は広島と長崎についての詩をかなり書きました。私はそのひとつを皆様と共に分かち合いたいと思います。題は「空のこだま」です。詩は伊藤一長前長崎市長

120

の言葉の引用で始まります。

空のこだま

「今日長崎の鐘の音よ空にこだませよ……」
　　　　——伊藤一長前長崎市長

長崎の空はつらく、青く、不屈のまま未来の約束を抱いている。街は私達をやさしく迎えるがかつては原爆の標的となった。雲が開いて隙間を作り破壊の惨劇が起こった。でも誰もが予期しないうちに花々が戻って来た。記憶は痛々しく時には耐えられない。謝罪の言葉はやっては来なかった。生存者たちは老いて力を失った。世代は遷る。海上の空は悲しみに満ちている。長崎の鐘よ響き渡れ、平和のために。空にこだませよ。

今回の私の長崎訪問は伊藤前市長が悲劇的な死を遂げてから初めての訪問です。私は

121

鮮やかに思い出します。彼は非常なる魅力と温かい心の持ち主でした。核兵器時代を終わらせるために活動し、また長崎の過去が他のいかなる都市の未来ともなってはならないと訴え続けた信念の人でした。世界中の多くの人々が市長の貢献に感謝しなければなりません。彼は私達の時代の中で緊急を要する核兵器問題の指導者でした。

長崎は魔法の街であると共に詩的な街です。約六十五年前の原子による破壊と荒廃の灰から長崎は立ち上がり、世界的な核脅威撤廃運動の指導都市となりました。この市民集会は核兵器廃絶の活動に一般市民に参加していただく模範です。長崎の鐘はこだまして空に抱かれます。鐘はあらゆる場所の人々に呼びかけて平和の精神と世界的な協調の精神を目覚めさせます。そして憎しみを許しと愛に変貌させる力を呼び覚まします。長崎は常に外国人が日本に入国する入り口です。それは日本から世界への門口でもあり、みなさんの伝言は世界が耳を傾けるべき重要な伝言であります。

私は四十年間核兵器廃絶の仕事をして来ました。財団の最初のしかも最も重要な目標は核兵器の廃以降は財団と共に活動して来ました。一九八一年の核時代平和財団の創立

絶です。私達はまた国際法を強化し平和活動の指導者となる新たな世代を育成したいと努力しています。二つの目的は手を繋ぎ合って共に歩みます。核兵器の廃絶は国際法の強化と若い世代の指導者の育成なしには達成出来ません。それゆえ私達はこの恐ろしい兵器の完全な撤廃を国際法と合致させる方向で断固として要求していくべきです。平和の指導者となる新たな世代はこの要求に加わり、私達と共に肩を並べて立って欲しいのです。最後の核兵器が撤廃され破壊されるまで、若い指導者たちを教育し助言し活動に参加してもらわなければなりません。

「核兵器での地球破壊（オムニサイド）」と「核廃絶」についてお話したいと思います。

「地球破壊（オムニサイド）」とは哲学者ジョン・サマヴィルが作り出した用語です。それは自殺（スイサイド）と大量虐殺（ジェノサイド）の概念の延長です。それはすべての破壊、あらゆる破壊を意味します。核兵器は地球破壊の可能性を持ちます。核兵器はあらゆるものを破壊する力を持ちます――文明、人類、他の生物、芸術、音楽、記憶、詩、文学、過去、未来など。想像し得るいかなるものも核兵器で破壊され得ます、想像力そのものすら。なんと私達人間は賢いのでしょうか。私達人類は道具を作ることが出

来ました。そして私達と他の生命形を全滅させることが出来る道具を作ったのです。これは非常に恐ろしいことです。

地球上にある核兵器の数は人類のすべての生命を終わらせるに十分であることには疑問の余地はありません。この危険を何が正当化出来るでしょうか？　この危険を冒し続けることは狂気の沙汰ではないでしょうか？　政治の指導者たちがこのことを理解していないように思われるのは何故でしょうか？　変革への指導者はどこにいるのでしょうか？

一筋の希望の光はバラク・オバマがアメリカの大統領となったことです。彼は「核兵器の無い世界の平和と安全保障」を求めます。ですがオバマは私達に告げました、彼はさほど楽天的ではなく、このことは達成されそうにもないことであると。彼は私達に諭しました、忍耐が必要であると。ですが忍耐は核拡散を助長させ、さらなる核兵器による大惨事に至らせる可能性があります。それを彼が理解していたら目標をより緊急な切迫感でたとえ少しずつでも早めはしなかったでしょうか？

もう一筋の希望の光は国連事務総長のバン・ギムン氏です。彼はすべての集団を核拡散防止条約（NPT）に招き、「条約が要求するように、新たな協定あるいは信頼し得る検証制度に基づいた相互的な補強手段により、核廃絶への信念を持って交渉を追求」しました。これは国際的に最高位の行政事務官からの指導力として着目すべきです。

地球市民としての私達の任務は強力な声となることです。オバマ大統領やバン・ギムン氏のように廃絶を求める指導者たちは支援の固い基盤を持つと感じるでしょう。そして人類の脅威である核兵器を切迫感を持って撤廃させる強さを彼らに与えるでしょう。

私達には私達に与えられた仕事があります。目標の達成には困難を伴います、これは明らかです。私達の相手は強大な権力です。私達の要求を彼らに聞かせなければなりません。十九世紀の奴隷解放運動のフレデリック・ダグラスが「権力は要求なしでは何も譲歩しない。譲歩したことはないし今後もしないだろう」と述べた通りです。

私達はオバマ大統領に多大な緊急感を持って行動する勇気を与えねばなりません。で すがまた金正日氏が核拡散防止条約の協議の場に来て、安全保障の確証と開発途上国援 助と引き替えに彼の核兵器を諦めて北東アジア非核地帯条約に加盟してくれるように勇 気付ける必要があります。また被爆者の霊を協議の場へ連れ出さなければなりません。 もしこれが可能なら憎しみを愛と許しへ変貌させる力を行使出来ます。そして変革され た「思考規範」を反映する新しいエネルギーを協議の場に注ぎ込むことが出来ます。思 考規範の変革、アルバート・アインシュタインはそれを「比類のない惨事」を回避する に絶対に必要なものと考えました。

　広島と長崎の被爆者たちは生涯に渡る痛みと苦しみの証拠を語ってくれました。被爆 者の声を空と地球上すべてにこだまさせましょう。　私はみなさんにこの市民集会から五 つの行動をお願いしたいのです。

　まず初めに、オバマ大統領と世界の他の指導者たちを長崎市に招いてください。彼ら にまず核の力による壊滅がどういうものか見てもらい、その姿から許しと愛に変貌させ

る力を引き出してもらいたいのです。

第二に、二〇一〇年の核拡散防止条約再検討会議に強力な被爆者代表団を送り、それぞれの代表に会議の参加者たちに緊急感を持って核兵器の廃絶に努力するよう訴えて欲しいのです。

第三に、被爆者の代表を世界中に送って彼らの話を若い人々に聞かせ、若い人々がこの集会のアピールを分かち合って核兵器撤廃のために努力する参加者たちを共に励ますようになって欲しいのです。

第四に、日本政府にアメリカの核の傘から抜け出ることを訴え、核抑止の拡大に政府が依存していることを止めさせて欲しいのです。

第五に、広島と長崎の被爆者たちへのノーベル平和賞を訴え続けて欲しいのです。オバマ大統領は彼が為すかもしれない行為によって受賞しました。被爆者たちこそ今まで

に「二度と原爆を使うな！」と力強く訴え続けて来た活動によって受賞に値します。

次に私は五月に行われる二〇一〇年核拡散防止条約再検討会議を中心にお話したいと思います。会議への参加国は熟慮の上に以下の事項を記憶に留めて狭い有利性よりも核兵器の脅威に向けた総合的な解決を求めるべきです。

・核兵器は現実のしかも現在の時点で地球上の人類と他の生命を脅かし続けています。

・一ケ国の安全保障に基づき罪のない何億もの人々、恐らくは何十億もの人々を殺害する脅威と文明破壊の危険とはいかなる道徳的な正当化も持たず最大の非難に値します。

・すべての核兵器廃絶のために現存する法的な諸義務を遂行することなしには核兵器の拡散を防止することは不可能です。

・核エネルギーの施設が世界中に拡がれば、核拡散の防止と核兵器の廃絶の達成は共に不可能とは言えないまでもはるかに困難となるでしょう。

・世界全体が核兵器による脅威を撤廃する方向に歩むためには、現在そして未来の世代に対する現在の核兵器の拡大し過ぎた危険について新たな考え方が必要となります。

核時代平和協会は次の五つの優先行動を二〇一〇年の核拡散防止条約再検討会議での協定に向けて支持します。

1. 条約に加盟したそれぞれの核保有国は保有する核兵器の数を正確にまた公的に発表し、それを使用した場合、地球環境と人間とにいかなる破壊力を及ぼすかを査定して核兵器廃絶に向けての手段を工夫し明言すべきです。

2. 条約に加盟したすべての核保有国はそれぞれの安全保障政策における核兵器の役割を削減すべきです。核保有国は高度に危険な状態にあるすべての核の力を低減させ他の核保有国に対して最初に核兵器を使用することを禁じ、核を持たない国に対しては使用を禁じるように誓って欲しいのです。

3. 軍事目的あるいは非軍事目的とにかかわらず、すべての濃縮ウランと再生プルトニウムそしてそれらの製造施設（すべてのウラニウム濃縮とプルトニウム分離技術を含める）は厳格で効果ある国際的な安全管理の下に置かれるべきです。

4. すべての条約加盟国は核拡散防止条約の第五条を再考し平和目的のための核エネル

129

ギーの「剝奪し得ない権利」の促進に原子力発電による核拡散問題を考慮するべきです。（訳者注・「剝奪し得ない権利」＝アメリカ独立宣言文の一句、「生命、自由、幸福の追求」を指す）

5. すべての条約加盟国は段階的な、嘘偽りもない、撤回不可能なしかも透明な核兵器廃絶のための核兵器禁止条約採択に向けて協議を開始するべきです。そして一九九六年の「世界法廷助言的意見」によって補強され明文化された核拡散防止条約の第六条に従い二〇一五年までに協議を完了すべきです。

（訳者注・「核兵器禁止条約」＝二〇〇七年四月コスタリカ・マレーシア両政府の共同提案として国連に提出された。いまだ完全に採択されてはいない。「世界法廷助言的意見」＝一九九六年七月八日付けでハーグ国際司法裁判所によって助言として提示された「核兵器の威嚇あるいは使用に関する合法性」を指す）

核拡散防止条約再検討会議の最も重要な行動は核兵器禁止条約に向けて友好的な協議を開始することへの合意でしょう。その合意は核兵器撤廃の世界へ前進する国々が必要とする政治的な意志を表明するでありましょう。もしアメリカが協議を召集する指導者

130

となり得なければ日本が指導的な役割を担って欲しいのです。しかしながら、どの国々が指導権を握ろうとも全体協議の開始会議は広島で開催されるように提案します。広島は核による破壊を経験した最初の都市です。そして最終会議は長崎で開催されることを提案します。長崎は核による被害を経験した第二番目の都市でありますし、私は最後の都市であることを希望します。

もし合意声明が新たな条約すなわち核兵器禁止条約採決への協議を開始するに至れば、私達は核兵器撤廃の世界へ向けて貴重な道のりを歩み始めることになります。広島と長崎の被爆者は彼らの訴えが聞き届けられたと知るに足る道でありましょう。

もうひとつの詩を共に分かち合ってください。「長崎の鐘」です。

長崎の鐘

長崎の鐘は

苦しんだ者のために鳴る
そしていまだ苦しむ者のために

鐘の音は引きつける　老いた女を
愛に輝く目をした
若い二人を

誘う　幼い子供達を
懸命に歩いて行く
爆心地へ向かって

長崎の鐘の音は
流れゆく　河のように
鳴れ　私達すべてのために　鳴れ
降りしきる落ち葉のように

ありがとうございます。長崎の鐘は世界中に響き渡ると確信しようではありませんか。

決して希望を失ってはなりません。より安全でより正気の世界、すべての核兵器廃絶の

世界に向けての努力を決して諦めてはなりません。

（「第四回核兵器廃絶――地球市民集会ナガサキ」開会集会でのスピーチ、

於・長崎市、二〇一〇年二月六日）

石炭袋

デイヴィッド・クリーガー詩集
『神の涙——広島・長崎原爆　国境を越えて』増補版

2010 年 8 月 6 日　初版発行
2020 年 2 月 27 日　増補版発行

著　者　　　デイヴィッド・クリーガー
訳　者　　　水崎野里子
編集・発行者　鈴木比佐雄
発行所　　　株式会社 コールサック社

〒 173-0004　東京都板橋区板橋 2-63-4-209
電話 03-5944-3258　　FAX 03-5944-3238
suzuki@coal-sack.com　http://www.coal-sack.com
郵便振替 00180-4-741802
印刷管理　（株）コールサック社　制作部

装丁　亜久津歩

ISBN978-4-86435-424-0　C1092　￥1500E

DAVID KRIEGER 『God's Tears』
Reflections on the Atomic Bombs Dropped on Hiroshima and Nagasaki
The Additional Edition

Translated by Noriko Mizusaki
Published by Coal Sack Publishing Company

Coal Sack Publishing Company
2-63-4-209 Itabashi Itabashi-ku Tokyo 173-0004 Japan
Tel:（03）5944-3258 / Fax:（03）5944-3238
suzuki@coal-sack.com　http://www.coal-sack.com
President: Hisao Suzuki

CONTENTS

Ⅲ   MEMORY

Ⅳ THE CHALLENGE

Ⅴ OMNICIDE AND ABOLITION

AUTHOR

David Krieger is a founder of the Nuclear Age Peace Foundation and has served as its president since 1982. He has lectured throughout the United States, Europe and Asia on issues of peace, security, international law, and the abolition of nuclear weapons. He has received many awards for his work for a more peaceful and nuclear weapon-free world.

He has written extensively on nuclear dangers to humanity. His latest book, which he edited, is entitled *In the Shadow of the Bomb* (2018, Amazon). He is the author of two collections of poetry: *Today is Not a Good Day for War* (Santa Barbara, CA: Capra Press, 2005) and others.

Dr. Krieger is a councilor on the World Future Council and an advisor to many groups working for peace in the Nuclear Age. He holds a Ph.D. in Political Science from the University of Hawaii and a J.D. from the Santa Barbara College of Law.

He is one of the activists who dedicated himself for "The International Campaign to Abolish Nuclear Weapons" (ICAN), which won the Nobel Prize for Peace in 2017.

PREFACE

I first visited Hiroshima and Nagasaki shortly aftergraduating from college in 1963. Each city has created a Peace Memorial Museum that holds the memories of the human suffering caused by the atomic bombings. I was awakened and deeply moved by the horrific images I saw in these museums. For the most part, the story of the human suffering is not part of the American lore about the use of the bombs. That lore has been far simpler: "We dropped the bombs; we won the war." It has been, sadly, a story of technological triumph.

Visiting the Memorial Museums opened my eyes to a distinctly different and far more profound way of looking at nuclear weapons, providing insight into the vast differences in perspective between those who had been above the bombs and those beneath. These differences continue to constitute a chasm so great as to suggest parallel universes.

Those above the bombs, the victors, cele-

brated the technological achievement of their weapons. They went on to engage in a nuclear arms race based upon Mutually Assured Destruction (MAD). Those beneath the bombs, the victims, looked into the hellish inferno –the blast, fire and radiation – created by the detonation of the atomic bombs. They saw the consequences of the bombs displayed in death and devastation. They learned a far different lesson than had the victors: "Never again! We shall not repeat the evil."

The vision of humanity's future held by those above the bombs and those beneath the bombs may prove to be the decisive struggle of our time. On the side of technological triumph is the arrogance of power that is willing to put at risk the future of civilization, if not of life itself. On the side of the survivors, the hibakusha, is the moral clarity of calling evil by its name.

Resolving this struggle between technological "supremacy" and moral clarity has not been easy. Technology has been a driving force in modern societies and has been imbued with an aura of prestige. The joyous street celebrations by ordinary people in India and Pakistan after each country

tested nuclear weapons in 1998 remain vivid in my memory as testimony to the perceived prestige of becoming a nuclear power.

Many people on the planet are confused about nuclear weapons and feel disempowered in attempting to confront their dangers. Many are also ignorant, apathetic or in denial. Unfortunately, such orientations toward nuclear weapons are *de facto* votes for continuing, even escalating, the nuclear threat to humanity. Only by opposing nuclear weapons and working actively for their elimination can an individual align his or her perspective and action with the perspectives of those beneath the bombs, the Hiroshima and Nagasaki survivors, the most qualified ambassadors of the Nuclear Age.

I have returned many times to Hiroshima and Nagasaki, and I have always been encouraged by the indomitable spirit of the hibakusha. As time passes, they are growing older and need our help and support in spreading their powerful warning that human beings and nuclear weapons cannot coexist. I share their belief that we must choose: nuclear weapons or a human future. The choice should not

be difficult.

We humans created nuclear weapons and have tried to control them. We have not used them in warfare since the bombings of Hiroshima and Nagasaki on August 6 and 9, 1945 respectively. Sixty-five years have passed, and we have been fortunate not to again have had the fury of atomic destruction unleashed on our world. We should celebrate this good fortune, but not be satisfied with it. It falls to us – all of us – to demonstrate the courage and commitment it will require to dismantle and abolish nuclear weapons, creating a world we can be proud to pass on to future generations.

David Krieger
Santa Barbara, California

I

THE BOMB

THE SCIENTISTS

The scientists who developed the atomic bomb were in a race, or at least they thought so. They were saving the world from a Hitler bomb. But in May 1945, the war in Europe ended and Hitler was dead. The scientists never thought their creation would be used on Japan. Some of them, like Leo Szilard, tried hard to stop it from being used, except as a demonstration without people below. Some supported the bomb being used, but were never told that Japan was trying to surrender. The scientists made the most powerful bomb the world had yet known and, when it was made, the small men of politics took charge and sent them away. The moral of the story: Be careful for whom you build bombs.

LEO SZILARD

Strange little man with slicked-back black hair
and the best of intentions. One day you intuited
the Bomb while waiting at a red light in London.
Alarmed by the explosion in your mind you went
to your friend Einstein, warning him it could be a
Hitler Bomb. You asked Einstein to send a letter
to Roosevelt, and he did. That was the beginning.

Working under the bleachers at Hutchins' Univer-
sity you helped give shiny metallic life to your idea,
but your conscience stopped you short when you
knew they were going to drop it. You wrote to Truman
who sent you to Byrnes who scorned you. You shiv-
ered as your train rolled homeward, knowing you
had lost control forever of your demon child.

AFTER TRINITY

In the week after the Trinity test,
which lit up the early morning sky
with its fierce white power,
Oppenheimer was somber.

Knowing what was soon to follow,
he walked aimlessly about Los Alamos
puffing on his pipe, his eyes vacant.

Over and over, he muttered,
"Those poor little people, those poor
little people."

PAUL TIBBETS

You were a pilot, a kid, a cog, a boy, a bomber. You flew your plane into history from Tinian Island to Hiroshima. Nearly everyone has heard of the famous plane, *Enola Gay*, the one you named for your mother, the one that carried the Bomb that day to Hiroshima.

You swore you served a noble cause, and saved the lives of American boys. Others, like my now dead father-in-law, who fought in the Pacific, thought so too. In the deep of night you had no second thoughts, no guilt or might-have-beens. Soldiers salute, and you saluted and flew the *Enola Gay* and never looked back.

HIROSHIMA, AUGUST 6, 1945

It was a clear sky, the air tingled
with heat and promise,
as men and women set off for work
and children kissed their mothers goodbye.

As the bomb drifted toward earth
city people walked with small steps
along narrow roads, across graceful bridges
on their way to oblivion.

The shadow of the bomb slipped away
from time, escaping the roar and blast
and cruel heat that stopped the city.

AUGUST MORNINGS

Hiroshima

Clear summer morning —
The steel-hearted bomb
Just a speck in the sky

Nagasaki

The bomb shatters
The humid summer silence —
Severs the heads of stone saints

THE FOUR SEASONS OF HIROSHIMA

Summer
A quiet morning
Suddenly the sun explodes

Autumn
The people wander
Through the ash

Winter
Without the sun
The cold penetrates

Spring
The grasses return
And the plum blossoms

YOSUKE YAMAHATA

The day the bomb fell on Nagasaki, you were there
with your camera, capturing evidence of the crime.

Click. A dying infant sucking at her mother's breast,
the mother's eyes glazed and distant.

Click. A dazed child holding a rice ball, her eyes
blank, her face covered with scratches.

Click. The rigid body of a charred young boy
stretched out and blackened on the crisp earth,

one hand clutching at his chest, the other hand
twisted in a strange way, his face passive.

A SHORT HISTORY LESSON: 1945

August 6th:
Dropped atomic bomb
On civilians
At Hiroshima.

August 8th:
Agreed to hold
War crimes trials
For Nazis.

August 9th:
Dropped atomic bomb
On civilians
At Nagasaki.

GOD RESPONDED WITH TEARS

The plane flew over Hiroshima and dropped the
bomb after the all clear warning had sounded.

The bomb dropped far slower than the speed of
light. It dropped at the speed of bombs.

From the ground it was a tiny silver speck
that separated from the silver plane.

After 43 seconds, the slow falling bomb exploded
into mass at the speed of light squared.

Einstein called it energy. Everything lit up.
For a split-second people could see their own bones.

The pilot always believed he had done the right
thing. The President, too, never wavered from his
belief.

He thanked God for the bomb. Others did, too.
God responded with tears that fell far slower

than the speed of bombs.
They still have not reached Earth.

EISENHOWER'S VIEW

*"It wasn't necessary to hit them
with that awful thing."*
        – General Dwight D. Eisenhower

We hit them with it, first
at Hiroshima and then at Nagasaki –
the old one-two punch.

The bombings were tests really, to see
what those "awful things" would do.

First, of a gun-type uranium bomb, and then
of a plutonium implosion bomb.

Both proved highly effective
in the art of obliterating cities.

It wasn't necessary.

THE BOMB

The Bomb, a tear falling from its metallic eye, is more than just a bomb.

It is a surrender of sanity, a longing for the darkness and the calm.

II

THE SURVIVORS

THE PEOPLE BENEATH

At the center of the city
The people were incinerated
Becoming ashes in the wind
With glowing red edges.
No longer holding memories
But becoming memories –
Drifting with the clouds.

At the edges of the city
The people survived longer,
Holding memories of the moment
In their bones and hearts,
Which became brittle and sad.

The survivors were sorrowful
And did their best to remind us
Of the new elements in the wind,
But their voices were soft
And it was a busy time on Earth.

FORGIVE ME, MOTHER
for Shoji Sawada

After the bomb, the young boy
awakened beneath the rubble of his room.

He could hear his mother's cries,
still trapped within the fallen house.

He struggled to free her, but he lacked
the strength.

A fire raged toward them. Many people
hurried past.

Frightened and dazed, they would not stop
to help him free his mother.

He could hear her voice from the rubble.
The voice was soft but firm.

"You must run and save yourself,"
she told him. "You must go."

"Forgive me," he said, bowing,
"Forgive me, Mother."

He did as his mother wished.
That was long ago, in 1945.

The boy has long been a man, a good man.
Yet he still runs from those flames.

ARTIFACTS AND ASHES

Among the artifacts
were crisply charred bodies.

In one of the charred bodies
a daughter recognized
the gold tooth of her mother.

As the girl reached out
to touch the burnt body
her mother crumbled to ashes.

The ashes sifted through her hands
and floated to the ground.

The wind carried the ashes
to the four corners
of an unsettled world.

THE DEEP BOW OF A HIBAKUSHA
for Miyoko Matsubara

She bowed deeply. She bowed deeper than the oceans. She bowed from the top of Mt. Fuji to the bottom of the ocean. She bowed so deeply and so often that the winds blew hard.

The winds blew her whispered apologies and prayers across all the continents. But the winds whistled too loudly, and made it impossible to hear her apologies and prayers. The winds made the oceans crazy. The water in the oceans rose up in a wild molecular dance. The oceans threw themselves against the continents. The people were frightened. They ran screaming from the shores. They feared the white water and the whistling wind. They huddled together in dark places. They strained to hear the words in the wind.

In some places there were some people who thought they heard an apology. In other places there were people who thought they heard a prayer.

She bowed deeply. She bowed more deeply than anyone should bow.

A GRANDMOTHER'S STORY

The grandmother looked into the eyes
of her granddaughter, recalling the day
the bomb dropped on Hiroshima.

The sky was bluest blue, she said.
And when the sky exploded
the wind knocked me off my feet.

All around me there were screams
that still echo in my ears,
children calling for their mothers.

The wounded walked past us
With vacant stares, their skin hanging
like ribbons from their bodies.

Hiroshima became a city of death.
We lost all will to live until
new shoots of grass appeared.

With them, the darkness melted
into small green blades of hope.

PEOPLE OF THE BOMB

It began with fear, not famine.
What was missing was an understanding
of consequences.

Still, the sky held a blue-white innocence.
It would be many years before light
would become so intense that you could see
your bones through translucent skin.

Silos still held grain, not missiles.
Snow-capped mountains brushed the sky
and held it aloft.

The bomb may have ended the war, but only
if history is read like a distant star.

If only time had not bolted and changed course.
If only the white flags had flown before
the strange storm.

If only the sky had not turned white and aged.
If only there had been one less Einstein
and one more Vonnegut.

EINSTEIN'S REGRET

Einstein's regret ran deep
Like the pools of sorrow
That were his eyes.

His mind could see things
That others could not,
The bending of light,

The slowing of time,
Relationships of trains passing
In the night, and power,

Dormant and asleep,
That could be awakened,
But who would dare?

He saw patterns
In snowflakes and stars,
Unimaginable simplicity.

When the shadow of Hitler
Spread across Europe.
What was Einstein to do?

His regret ran deep, deeper
Than the pools of sorrow
That were his eyes.

WHERE DID THE VICTIMS GO?

Where else would the victims go but first into the air, then into the water, then into the grasses, and eventually into our food? I speak of the victims incinerated at Hiroshima and Nagasaki, those too close to the center who were caught in the heat and fire of our new power. I speak of the victims burned away to their elemental particles, to atoms, similar to other atoms, let loose into the atmosphere to drift and fall without volition.

What does this mean? That we breathe our victims, that we drink them and eat them, without tasting the bitterness, in our daily meals. It means there is no way to live without ourselves becoming in subtle and powerful ways those we have destroyed.

DANCE OF HIROSHIMA

With faltering steps
you became a child,
a maiden, a mother,
a widow, a mourner.
You stumbled and fell,
you picked yourself up,
grew wings and flew away.

I watched you dance
your fear and anger,
your youth and magic.
I watched you rise
from the ashes, fly
with the wings of a crane
and float back to Earth.

ON BECOMING DEATH

"Now I am become death, the destroyer of worlds."
                                    – Bhagavad Gita

When Oppenheimer thought, "Now *I am* become death," did he mean, "Now *we have* become death? Was Oppenheimer thinking about himself or all of us?

That August of '45 Truman and his military boys destroyed a few worlds. They never understood that among the worlds they destroyed was their own.

From Alamogordo to Hiroshima took exactly three weeks. On August 6th, Oppenheimer again became death. So did Groves, Stimson and Byrnes. So did Truman. So did a hundred thousand that day in Hiroshima. And so did America.

"This is the greatest thing in history," Truman said. He didn't think *he'd* become death *that* day. We Americans know how to win. Truman was a winner, *a destroyer of worlds.* Three days later, Truman and his military boys did it again at Nagasaki.

Sometime later, Oppenheimer visited Truman. "I have blood on my hands," Oppenheimer said. Truman didn't like those words.

Blood? What blood? When Oppenheimer left, Truman said, "Don't ever let him in here again."

HIBAKUSHA DO NOT JUST HAPPEN

For every *hibakusha*
there is a pilot

for every *hibakusha*
there is a planner

for every *hibakusha*
there is a bombardier

for every *hibakusha*
there is a bomb designer

for every *hibakusha*
there is a missile maker

for every *hibakusha*
there is a missileer

for every *hibakusha*
there is a targeter

for every *hibakusha*
there is a commander

for every *hibakusha*
there is a button pusher

for every *hibakusha*
many must contribute

for every *hibakusha*
many must obey

for every *hibakusha*
many must be silent

Ⅲ

MEMORY

AT THE HIROSHIMA PEACE MEMORIAL MUSEUM

A scale model of the city in August 1945 shows that the bomb exploded above Shima Hospital, 600 meters in the air, 300 meters southeast of its target, the Aioi Bridge. Within the range of the bomb were Honkawa Elementary School and five Buddhist temples: Jisanji, Denpukuji, Myouhoji, Joenji and Seiganji. As I walked through the museum, Japanese students in blue uniforms chattered. One young boy said to his classmate, "All this happened a very long time ago."

WHAT SHALL WE CALL THE BOMB DROPPED ON HIROSHIMA?

Shall we call it
Flash of White Light Maker or
Mushroom Cloud in Sky Maker?

Shall we call it
Terminator of War Bomb or
Incinerator of People Weapon?

Shall we call it
Secret Victory Weapon or
Dark Shadow Revealing Bomb?

Shall we call it
Rescuer of Young Soldiers Weapon or
Creator of Orphans Bomb?

Shall we call it
The Beginning of the End or
The End of the Beginning?

SADAKO AND THE SHAKUHACHI

We remember Hiroshima not for the past, but for
the future. We remember Hiroshima so that its
past will not become our future. Hiroshima is best
remembered with the plaintive sounds of the bam-
boo flute, the Shakuhachi. It conjures up the devas-
tation, the destruction, the encompassing emptiness
of that day. The Shakuhachi reveals the tear in the
fabric of humanity that was ripped open by the
bomb.

Nuclear weapons are not weapons at all. They are
a symbol of an imploding human spirit. They are
a fire that consumes the air of decency. They are a
crossroads where science joined hands with evil and
apathy. They are a triumph of academic certainty
wrapped in the convoluted lie of deterrence. They
are Einstein's regret. They are many things, but not
weapons -- not instruments of war, but of genocide
and perhaps of omnicide.

Those who gather to retell and listen to the story of Hiroshima and of Sadako are a community, a community committed to a human future. We may not know one another, but we are a community. And we are part of a greater community gathered throughout the world to commemorate this day, seeking to turn Hiroshima to Hope.

If we succeed, Sadako of a thousand cranes will be remembered by new generations. She will be remembered long after the names and spirits of those who made and used the bomb will have faded into the haunting sounds of the Shakuhachi.

AN IMPROBABLE GARDEN

Where I go, sad city, you go with me.
You are not worldly like Paris or Rome,
but neither am I.
You are not a city of snow-capped peaks,
nor one with the calm sea wrapped around you.
These wonders do not change the soul.
You are not New York, nor Delhi, nor Rio
with their milling throngs and excitement.
Such noise and light and busy-ness
are too ephemeral for you.

Your heritage is honorable. That counts
for something. After your tragedy
you clawed your own earth
until the plants slowly came back.
You are a city with the courage
to return from the dead.
Your people bow deeply and smile
their sorrowful smiles.

Hiroshima, sad city, I give you
the intensity of my solitude.
I give you the drumbeat of my heart.
I carry you with me in the hope
that from your spirit a better world
may one day blossom.
I give you the salt of my tears
to mix with your grief and promise.
Hiroshima, you are an improbable garden
and I, an even more improbable gardener.

ECHOES IN THE SKY

"Today the bells of Nagasaki echo in the sky…"
                            – Mayor Iccho Itoh, Nagasaki

The sky, bitter, blue, unyielding, holds promise.
The city, so welcoming,deserved far better. Clouds
opened making space for devastation. Before anyone
expected, the flowers returned. Memories are painful,
sometimes unbearable. Words of apology never came.
Survivors grow old and feeble. Generations pass.
The air above the sea is thick with sorrow. The bells
ring out for peace, echo in the sky.

THE BELLS OF NAGASAKI

The bells of Nagasaki
ring for those who suffered
and those who suffer still.

They draw old women to them
and young couples
with love-glazed eyes.

They draw in small children
walking awkwardly
toward the epicenter.

The bells of Nagasaki,
elusive as a flowing stream,
ring for each of us, ring
like falling leaves.

EARLY MORNING AT THE EPICENTER
Nagasaki, November 18, 2002

A chill is in the air this November morning.
Orange and yellow leaves tumble
Across neatly laid red bricks.

On nearby grass, groundskeepers, old men,
Rake the leaves into piles and gather them.
It is a gray morning, quiet and cold.

I stand in front of the epicenter,
Marked by a simple black monolith
Pointing skyward.

Five hundred meters above the monolith
The atomic bomb shuddered
and awakened long ago.

At the base of the monolith are flowers,
And nearby colorful folded cranes
Hang in tightly bunched clusters.

WHEN THE BOMB BECAME OUR GOD

When the bomb became our god
We loved it far too much,
Worshipping no other gods before it.

We thought ourselves great
And powerful, creators of worlds.

We turned toward infinity,
Giving the bomb our very souls.

We looked to it for comfort,
To its smooth metallic grace.

When the bomb became our god
We lived in a constant state of war
That we called *peace.*

DUCK AND COVER
- circa 1950

Children,
this is the way you will be saved
from a nuclear attack. At the sound
of the bell you will scramble as fast
as you can under your desk.
Face downward toward the floor
in a kneeling position
with your head resting on your arms.
Keep your eyes squeezed
tightly closed, not opening them
or looking up until you hear me say
"All clear."

This is the way you will be saved
from shards of glass and other objects
traveling at speeds of hundreds of miles
per hour. And from the flash of white
light that could melt your eyeballs. And

from the explosion that could scramble
your brains and the rest of your organs.
And this is the way you will be saved
from the fire that may incinerate you,
leaving you all shriveled, charred
and lifeless.

This is the way you will be saved
from the radiation that will cause your gums
to bleed, your hair to fall out, leukemia
to form in your blood, and lead
to either a slow and painful death,
or one more rapid and painful.
Pay close attention to the directions
so that you will get it right the first time.

CODE OF CONDUCT FOR NUCLEAR WEAPONS LAUNCH OFFICERS

I will not launch nuclear weapons unless I am ordered to do so.

I will turn my key when ordered to do so, no matter how many people will die.

I will sit in my silo and will not think for myself.

I will not worry that nuclear weapons kill indiscriminately and are equal opportunity destroyers.

I will ignore my obligations under international law, including the Nuremberg Principles.

I will prove I am a good citizen of [fill in the name of your country] by my willingness to annihilate [fill in the name of target country].

PARALLEL UNIVERSES

"If only I had known,
I would have become a watch maker."

             – Albert Einstein

In a parallel universe, Einstein
sits at his workbench making watches.
Light still curves around bodies of mass,
but the watch maker knows nothing of it.
He only makes watches, simple and precise.

IV

THE CHALLENGE

TEN REASONS TO ABOLISH NUCLEAR WEAPONS

They are long-distance killing machines incapable of discriminating between soldiers and civilians, the aged and the newly born, or between men, women and children.

They threaten the destruction of cities, countries and civilization; of all that is sacred, of all that is human, of all that exists.

They threaten to foreclose the future.

They make cowards of their possessors, and in their use there can be no decency or honor.

They are a false god, dividing nations into nuclear "haves" and "have-nots," bestowing unwarranted prestige and privilege on those that possess them.

They are a distortion of science and technology, twisting our knowledge of nature to destructive purposes.

They mock international law, displacing it with an allegiance to raw power.

They waste our resources on the development of instruments of annihilation.

They concentrate power and undermine democracy.

They corrupt our humanity.

THE FINAL PERIOD?

Scientists tell us that the universe was created with a "Big Bang" some 15 billion years ago. To represent this enormous stretch of time, we can imagine a 15,000 page book. It would be a very large and heavy book, some 50 times larger than a normal book. In this book, each page would represent one million years in the history of the universe. If there were 1,000 words on each page, each word would represent 1,000 years.

Most of the book would be about the expansion of the universe after the Big Bang. Our solar system would not occur in this history of the universe until page 10,500. It would take another 500 pages until the first primitive forms of life occurred on Earth some four billion years ago. The slow evolution of life would occupy the book nearly to its end. It would not be until page 14,997 that human-like creatures would appear on the planet, and it would not be until just ten words from the end of page

15,000 that human civilization would make its appearance.

The Nuclear Age, which began in 1945, would be represented by the final period, the punctuation mark on the last page of the 15,000 page book. This small mark at the end of the volume indicates where we are today: inheritors of a 15 billion year history with the capacity to destroy ourselves and most other forms of life with our technological achievements. It is up to us to assure that the page is turned and that we move safely into the future, free from the threat that nuclear weapons pose to humanity and all forms of life.

IMAGINATION AND NUCLEAR WEAPONS

Einstein believed that knowledge is limited, but imagination is infinite.

Imagine the soul-crushing reality of a nuclear war, with billions of humans dead; in essence, a global Hiroshima, with soot from the destruction of cities blocking warming sunlight. There would be darkness everywhere, temperatures falling into a new ice age, with crop failures and mass starvation.

With nuclear weapons poised on hair-trigger alert and justified by the ever-shaky hypothesis that nuclear deterrence will be effective indefinitely, this should not be difficult to imagine.

In this sense, our imaginations can be great engines for change.

In our current world, bristling with nuclear weapons and continuous nuclear threat, we stand at the brink of the nuclear precipice. The best case scenario from the precipice, short of beginning a process of

abolishing nuclear arms, is that we have the great good fortune to avoid crossing the line into nuclear war and blindly continue to pour obscene amounts of money into modernizing nuclear arsenals, while failing to meet the basic human needs of a large portion of the world's population

The only way out of this dilemma is for the leaders of the world to come to their senses and agree that nuclear weapons must be abolished in order to assure that these weapons will never again be used. Given the state of the world we live in, this is more difficult to imagine.

What steps would need to be taken to realize the goal of nuclear abolition?

First, we would need a treaty to ban nuclear weapons. Such a treaty was agreed to in 2017 by a majority of countries in the United Nations, the Treaty on the Prohibition of Nuclear Weapons (TPNW). The treaty is now in the process of being ratified and will enter into force when ratified by 50 countries. Unfortunately and predictably, none of the nine nuclear-armed countries have supported the TPNW,

and many have been overtly hostile to the treaty.

Second, negotiations would need to commence on nuclear disarmament by the nations of the world, including all nine of the nuclear-armed countries. The nuclear Non-Proliferation Treaty (NPT) already obliges its parties to undertake such negotiations in good faith. Specifically, it calls for negotiations to end the nuclear arms race at an early date and to achieve complete nuclear disarmament. The nuclear-armed states parties to the NPT have failed to fulfill these obligations since 1970 when the treaty entered into force.

Third, the negotiations would need to be expanded to encompass issues of general and complete disarmament, in order not to allow nuclear abolition to lead to conventional arms races and wars. Again, the states parties to the NPT are obligated to undertake such negotiations in good faith, but have not even begun to fulfill this obligation.

If we can use our imaginations to foresee the horrors of nuclear war, we should be able to take the necessary steps to assure that such a tragedy doesn't occur. Those steps have been set forth in the two

treaties mentioned above.

What remains missing is the political will to implement the treaties. Without this political will, our imaginations notwithstanding, we will stay stuck in this place of potential nuclear catastrophe, where nuclear war can ensue due to malice, madness, miscalculation, mistake or manipulation (hacking). Imagination is necessary, but not sufficient, to overcome political will. Even treaties are not sufficient unless there is the political will to assure their provisions are implemented. To do this, imagination must be linked to action to demand a change in political will.

The time is short, the task is great, and terrible consequences are foreseeable if we continue to be stuck at the nuclear precipice

To do nothing is simply unimaginable.

THE PRESIDENT

Not the first American president
to govern by lies and misdirection,
he is cunningly adept at it.

Brazenly focused on himself,
he feeds his ego and stuffs his pockets
with emoluments.

He makes the world safe for bigots,
opening wide the spigots
of prejudice.

Creating violent waves
that crash against the poor, he strips
lady liberty of her honor.

He shouts "fake news"
and stands to gain at the public trough
like no previous president.

Each day brings new disgrace,

yet somehow he has managed
to hold on.

Like all tyrants, he will fall.
Question is: when he does, will we
still have a country and a world?

V

OMNICIDE AND ABOLITION

OMNICIDE AND ABOLITION
Speech in Nagasaki
February 6,2010

It is a great pleasure to be again in Nagasaki. Thank you all for welcoming us so warmly to your beautiful city. I have always been struck by the chance nature of the bombing of Nagasaki. The target of the bomb that fateful day was another city, Kokura, but clouds prevented the bombing of that city. If it hadn't been for those clouds, Nagasaki might never have been bombed. If there had not been a break in the clouds over Nagasaki, the city might never have been bombed. Something as ordinary as clouds can change our lives in profound ways. But so can our actions to build a world of peace and to eliminate nuclear weapons from our planet.

Over the years I have written a number of poems about Hiroshima and Nagasaki. I would like to share one of these, entitled "Echoes in the Sky." It begins with a quote by the former mayor of Nagasaki, Iccho Itoh.

ECHOES IN THE SKY

"Today the bells of Nagasaki echo in the sky…"
—Mayor Iccho Itoh, Nagasaki

The sky, bitter, blue, unyielding, holds promise.
The city, so welcoming, deserved far better.
Clouds opened making space for devastation.
Before anyone expected, the flowers returned.
Memories are painful, sometimes unbearable.
Words of apology never came. Survivors grow old
and feeble. Generations pass. The air above
the sea is thick with sorrow. The bells ring out
for peace, echo in the sky.

This is the first time I have been in Nagasaki
since the tragic death of Mayor Itoh. I remember him
vividly as a man of great charm and warmth. He had a
deep commitment to ending the nuclear weapons era
and to assuring that Nagasaki's past does not become
any other city's future. Many of us throughout the
world feel a debt of gratitude for the leadership he
provided on this most critical issue of our time.

Nagasaki is a city at once magical and poetic.
From the ashes of atomic devastation nearly 65 years
ago, Nagasaki has arisen to become a leading global

city in the movement for a world free of nuclear threat. These Citizens' Assemblies are models of engagement to involve ordinary citizens in the task of abolishing nuclear weapons. The bells of Nagasaki echo in the sky's embrace. These bells send forth a call to people everywhere to awaken to the spirit of peace, to global cooperation and the transformative powers of forgiveness and love. Nagasaki has always been an entry point for foreigners into Japan. It has also been a gateway outward to the world, and your message is one that is critical for the world to hear.

I have worked for nuclear disarmament for four decades, and have done so with the Nuclear Age Peace Foundation since its founding in 1982. Our first and most important goal at the Foundation is the abolition of nuclear weapons. We also seek to strengthen international law and to empower new generations of peace leaders. These goals go together hand-in-hand. We will not achieve abolition without strengthening international law and empowering new generations of peace leaders. So we need to be firm in our demands for the total abolition of these monstrous weapons in accord with international law, and new generations of peace leaders must join in this demand and stand with us shoulder-to-shoulder. We

need to educate and mentor young leaders to carry forward this struggle until the last nuclear weapon is dismantled and destroyed.

I would like to talk to you about Omnicide and Abolition. Omnicide is a term coined by the philosopher John Somerville. It is an extension of the concepts of suicide and genocide. It means the death of all, of everything. Nuclear weapons have the potential for omnicide. They could destroy everything – civilization, the human species, other forms of life, art, music, memory, poetry, literature, the past, the future. Anything you can imagine can be destroyed by nuclear weapons, even imagination itself. How clever we humans are. We are a tool-creating species, and we have created tools with which we are capable of annihilating ourselves and other forms of life. This should be a frightening thought to all of us.

There is no doubt that the number of nuclear weapons on our planet is sufficient to end human life. What can justify this risk? Is it not insane to continue to run this risk? Why does this seem to be something that our political leaders cannot see? Where is the leadership for change?

One ray of hope is Barack Obama assuming the presidency of the United States. He seeks "the peace and security of a world without nuclear weapons." But he tells us that he is not naive, and that this is not likely to be achieved in his lifetime. He tells us we must be patient. But if he knew that patience might make nuclear proliferation more likely and lead to further nuclear catastrophes, would he not instill his goal with a greater sense of urgency?

Another ray of hope is UN Secretary-General Ban Ki-moon, who has called for all parties to the Non-Proliferation Treaty "to pursue negotiations in good faith – as required by the treaty – on nuclear disarmament either through a new convention or through a series of mutually reinforcing instruments backed by a credible system of verification." This is important leadership coming from the top international civil servant.

Our task as global citizens is to become a strong enough voice that leaders seeking abolition, like President Obama and Ban Ki-moon, will feel a solid base of support behind them, providing them with the strength to seek to end the nuclear weapons

threat to humanity with a sense of urgency.

We have our work cut out for us. There is no doubt it will be difficult to achieve our goal. We face powerful forces. We must make our demands heard. As the 19th century anti-slavery abolitionist, Frederick Douglass, said: "Power concedes nothing without a demand. It never has and it never will."

We must encourage President Obama to act with greater urgency, but we must also encourage Kim Jong-Il to come to the negotiating table, give up his nuclear weapons in exchange for security assurances and development assistance, and join a Northeast Asia Nuclear Weapons-Free Zone. We must also bring the spirit of the hibakusha to the negotiating table. If we can do this, we can use the transforming powers of forgiveness and love to infuse the negotiations with a new energy reflective of the changed "modes of thinking" that Albert Einstein saw as essential to avert "unparalleled catastrophe."

The hibakusha of Hiroshima and Nagasaki have given testimony to enough pain and suffering for many lifetimes. Let their voices echo in the sky and throughout the Earth. I would ask you to take five

actions from this Citizens' Assembly.

First, invite President Obama and other world leaders to visit your city. Help them to see at first hand the nature of the nuclear power of annihilation and compare that to the transformative powers of forgiveness and love.

Second, send a strong delegation of hibakusha to the 2010 Non-Proliferation Treaty Review Conference and lobby each of the delegates to the conference, encouraging them to approach the elimination of nuclear weapons with a sense of urgency.

Third, send delegations of hibakusha throughout the world to tell their stories to young people, to share with them the Appeal that will come from this Assembly, and to encourage their leadership in the struggle for a world without nuclear weapons.

Fourth, lobby the Japanese government to step out from under the US nuclear umbrella and to end its reliance on extended nuclear deterrence.

Fifth, continue to lobby for a Nobel Peace Prize for the hibakusha of Hiroshima and Nagasaki.

President Obama received the prize for what he might do; the hibakusha deserve the prize for what they have done in powerfully spreading the message, "Never again!"

Now I would like to focus on the 2010 Non-Proliferation Treaty Review Conference, which will take place in May. In their deliberations, states parties to the conference should bear in mind the following in seeking a comprehensive solution to the threat of nuclear weapons rather than narrow advantage:

- Nuclear weapons continue to present a real and present danger to humanity and other life on Earth.
- Basing the security of one's country on the threat to kill tens of millions of innocent people, perhaps billions, and risking the destruction of civilization, has no moral justification and deserves the strongest condemnation.
- It will not be possible to prevent proliferation of nuclear weapons without fulfilling existing legal obligations for total nuclear disarmament.
- Preventing nuclear proliferation and achieving nuclear disarmament will both be made far more difficult, if not impossible, by expanding nuclear

energy facilities throughout the world.

- Putting the world on track for eliminating the existential threat posed by nuclear weapons will require new ways of thinking about this overarching danger to present and future generations.

The Nuclear Age Peace Foundation supports the following five priority actions for agreement at the 2010 NPT Review Conference:

1. Each signatory nuclear weapon state should provide an accurate public accounting of its nuclear arsenal, conduct a public environmental and human assessment of its potential use, and devise and make public a roadmap for going to zero nuclear weapons.

2. All signatory nuclear weapon states should reduce the role of nuclear weapons in their security policies by taking all nuclear forces off high-alert status, pledging No First Use of nuclear weapons against other nuclear weapon states and No Use against non-nuclear weapon states.

3. All enriched uranium and reprocessed plutonium – military and civilian – and their production facilities (including all uranium enrichment and

plutonium separation technology) should be placed under strict and effective international safeguards.

4. All signatory states should review Article IV of the NPT, promoting the "inalienable right" to nuclear energy for peaceful purposes, in light of the nuclear proliferation problems posed by nuclear electricity generation.

5. All signatory states should comply with Article VI of the NPT, reinforced and clarified by the 1996 World Court Advisory Opinion, by commencing negotiations in good faith on a Nuclear Weapons Convention for the phased, verifiable, irreversible and transparent elimination of nuclear weapons, and complete these negotiations by the year 2015.

The most important action by the NPT Review Conference would be an agreement to commence good faith negotiations for a Nuclear Weapons Convention. Such an agreement would demonstrate the needed political will among the world's countries to move forward toward a world without nuclear weapons. If the United States fails to lead in convening these negotiations, I would urge Japan to do so. Regardless of which countries provide the leadership, however,

I would propose that the opening session of these negotiations be held in Hiroshima, the first city to have suffered nuclear devastation, and the final session of these negotiations be held in Nagasaki, the second and, hopefully, last city to have suffered atomic devastation.

If agreement could be reached to begin these negotiations for a new treaty, a Nuclear Weapons Convention, we would be on a serious path toward a nuclear weapons-free world, one that would allow the hibakusha of Hiroshima and Nagasaki to know that their pleas have been heard.

I would like to conclude by sharing another poem, "The Bells of Nagasaki."

THE BELLS OF NAGASAKI

The bells of Nagasaki
ring for those who suffered
and those who suffer still.

They draw old women to them
and young couples
with love-glazed eyes.

They draw in small children
walking awkwardly
toward the epicenter.

The bells of Nagasaki,
elusive as a flowing stream,
ring for each of us, ring
like falling leaves.

Let's make sure that the echoes of the Nagasaki bells are heard throughout the world. Never lose hope, and never give up the struggle for a safer and saner world, free of all nuclear weapons.